FOLKTALES OF ANCIENT INDIA

Raywat Deonandan

Intanjible Publishing

IntanjiblePublishing

Dedicated to my late father, who I'm sure would have read these tales with fascination, and retold them with much animated joy.

CONTENTS

INTRODUCTION: THIS BOOK'S 25 YEAR JOURNEY TO PUBLICATION

The historic India comprises, in addition to the modern nation that bears its name, the countries and peoples of Pakistan, Bangladesh, Maldives, Nepal and Myanmar. If a single word could describe this ancient place, it would certainly be "diversity." India's variety, both cultural and linguistic, is such that it is more akin to a continent like Europe than to any single country.

With scores of living languages to support it, India's tradition of storytelling has grown to subtend a body of literature as potent and as relevant as any collection of classical European fairy tales.

Unlike Europe, however, India still draws from the rural purity of village life, an existence that describes a majority of its population. As its literacy rate is low compared to Western countries, in some rural communities India's ancient tradition of oral storytelling thrives in almost pristine condition to this day.

In 1919, scholar W. Norman Brown estimated that there were about 3000 oral tales available in India. Given the lesser extent of Western scholarly penetration in that era, Brown's was probably an underestimation. India's vast panoply of religions and movements has compelled the creation of countless myths and aphorisms to support those beliefs. It is from there that this great fountain of narrative erupts. Mythologies of all human cultures embody philosophies, while folktales present personal paradigms and themes, and impart a sort of common wisdom that serves as a single brick in the grand monolith of mythology.

In the Indian case, it is entirely possible that many instances of folk literature arose from a need of priests to convey, in accessible terms, the more esoteric aspects of their philosophies --aspects that sweeping mythology seems unable to communicate. Yet, as in the case of European literature, the piety and pomp of Indian religions are often torn away by their folk brethren to reveal a ribald core as guttural as Chaucer's *Canterbury Tales*. This is doubtless a manifestation of the oral foundation of Indian folk literature, one in which the people must be entertained before they can be placated by the socializing influence of the aforementioned philosophies.

The oral tradition is a valued one in the Indian subcontinent where one's erudition is sometimes determined as much by articulateness as by the letters after one's name. The power of language to convey both idea and status is reflected in the need for Indian public figures to display outstanding eloquence, more so than their Western counterparts; the requirement of great feats of recitation from school children of all ages; the resounding global success of modern Indian literature; and in the demarcation of ethnic and political boundaries along linguistic lines.

To Western ears, the recitation of Indian folk tales is a strangely comforting experience, made so for its familiar reference points: monsters to be conquered, talking animals, vengeful gods, beautiful princesses, noble princes and rags-to-riches yarns of all variety. The continuum of Indo-European culture is one that allows for these commonalities, but not so much so that Indian folk tales cannot introduce a novel sense of entertainment and fulfilment for the casual reader.

These tales originate from an oral tradition where travellers or elders would gather a community together beneath the stars and engage in a soothing theatrical and lyrical presentation. With each re-telling, the stories gather additional narrative, becoming more circuitous to support the drama of the live recitation. Some tales are derived from the Hindu epics, the *Ramayana* and the *Mahabharata*, and are therefore rife with moralization and deific references. Others may pre-date the Aryan influence and hearken to an older era.

Previous attempts to anthologize Indian folk tales have been of three varieties: the re-creation of the oral tale in its circuitous complexity, retaining a high degree of academic worth; the conveyance of Hindu philosophies, often using Biblical language and a Victorian ethic; or the modernization of the tales, carrying forward Aesopian lessons to all epochs and characterizations. The casual Western reader is perhaps most drawn to the latter category for its accessibility.

With this collection, I have endeavoured to adopt the oral storyteller's persona, wishing to entertain rather than to educate, while hoping to do both. Toward that end, these stories have been stripped of all inappropriate and circuitous side-plots, and their core narratives further developed. Where other anthologizers would have some of these tales convey a moral, I have chosen instead to remove any sense of judgement where one is unimportant to the flavour of the story. Unnecessary references to India's vast pantheon of gods and goddesses have been pruned since, in my belief, such references were sometimes added by Vedic storytellers to make pre-Aryan stories palatable to Hindu tastes.

Lastly, I admit to having altered the plots of a few of these tales to preserve a greater sense of irony and denouement. As this is not meant to be a scholarly work accurately portraying the history of Indian folk literature, I make no apologies for exercising my literary licence in this manner. As pointed out by the great Indian folk anthologizer, A.K. Ramanujan, even the Grimm Brothers rewrote and "embroidered" their "household tales."

Through many caffeine-filled hours in the stacks of imposing university libraries, poring over anthropological and historical tomes, I identified twenty-seven tales to anthologize herein. Over the years, I have found opportunity to tell some of them to gathered audiences in India, Trinidad, and Canada, adopting the role of the ancient oral storyteller. I'm pleased to report that they were well received by live audiences, with "Harisharam the Frog" being a particular crowd pleaser.

I first collected this volume in 1999, with the first draft of this introduction written on January 5th of that year. I revisited the collection on New Year's Day of 2016, intending then to do a comprehensive edit. But it was not until the middle of 2024 that I finally found the time and energy to bring it all to press. This book, however slight, might be a laborious twenty-five years in the making. But its stories are many centuries older, and will surely live on for many centuries hence.

Raywat Deonandan

BOPOLUCHI

In the northern state called Punjab, there lived a poor but beautiful girl named Bopoluchi. A kinder and warmer girl could not be imagined, blessed as well with joyful eyes and a magnificent mane of dark brown hair. But as sweet and as lovely as she was, it was unlikely that Bopoluchi would ever marry, since her father was quite destitute and therefore could not afford the dowry that most prospective grooms demanded.

Now, the village in which they lived was pestered by a devious robber who had become outrageously wealthy from having plundered many villages over his years. Despite his wealth, his ugliness and evilness had prevented him from obtaining a woman's hand in marriage. And marriage is what he desired. So, when he saw the lovely Bopoluchi playing with her friends, he conspired to steal her away as his wife.

The robber went to Bopoluchi's father, claiming to be a long-lost brother of Bopoluchi's dead mother, so devious and shameless was his robber's mind. He claimed that he had arranged for her to marry a handsome young man in a neighbouring village. Bopoluchi's father was pleased, of course, for he wished nothing but fulfilment for his beloved only daughter. But he hung his head in disappointment, pointing out that he could yet not afford the dowry that such a young man would require.

The robber smiled broadly and played his artifice to its fullest; "I shall be proud to pay her dowry, brother," he said. "It's the least I can do for my poor sister's only child."

Although Bopoluchi and her father were saddened to be parted, they both knew that this was a rare opportunity for her to escape her poverty. Sadly and gratefully, they accepted the offer.

One can only imagine the bittersweet sentiment that must have gripped Bopoluchi's heart: to be taken from her friends and father --all the joy and comfort she had ever known-- toward an unknown future whose only guarantee was a degree of financial comfort. Yet there was no doubt that it was the right thing to do.

So, the next morning, the robber and Bopoluchi set out for the fictitious neighbouring village. As the carriage pulled away, Bopoluchi felt her home receding behind her back. With each passing tree, the path became newer and stranger. And with the passing hours, the face of her "uncle" slipped from uneasy grace to the face of deception and wickedness.

Now, many miles away from the village, the robber revealed his true identity, confessing that he intended to marry Bopoluchi himself. Bopoluchi recoiled in horror. Her first instinct was to flee from the carriage into the unknown woods, but could not escape the robber's strong grip. He held his captive firmly by her wrists, conveying well the certainty of her unfortunate destiny: she would be his wife, whether or not she wanted him. er tears blurred her vision, and she was too overcome with terror and shock to offer any sort of resistance, not even a scream. Her plight seemed to darken further as the robber pulled Bopoluchi from the carriage and forced her into the dark woods.

He dragged her to a little hovel hidden deep within the forest. In the hovel lived the robber's terrifying old mother, a bald witch whose nasty temperament and spiteful manner matched well her hideous features and foul odour. The robber left Bopoluchi to be guarded by the witch while he set out to make the wedding arrangements.

While the robber was away, the witch tormented Bopoluchi with dire predictions for her future. She told the girl of how she would slave away her days in servitude, tending to all the robber's needs, never seeing the outside world except to fetch water to clean the robber's stash of gold and jewels. She spoke cruelly of the father Bopoluchi would never see again, and of the joyful and innocent life she would never again lead. The bald witch then extracted from a chest the wedding dress she had prepared for

Bopoluchi; it was equipped with straps, buckles and chains for securing the bride lest she attempt to run away.

Bopoluchi realized then that no rescue could ever be forthcoming, and she was not strong enough to fight either the robber or the cold crone. She must escape using her guile. Better to die in an attempt than to contemplate an awful life in this horrific family.

When the witch brought out the wedding dress, she noticed for the first time the long lush hair with which Bopoluchi had been blessed. "Tell me, wicked child," the old crone said, "how did you get such long hair?"

"When my mother was alive," Bopoluchi answered, "she would hold my head against a stone and pound it with a pestle. In that way, my scalp was stimulated and encouraged to grow thick hair."

The crone was intrigued, of course, since she herself had lost all her hair years ago. "If you'd like," Bopoluchi offered, "I could give your scalp the same treatment!"

Overcome with vanity and pride, the crone agreed, and placed her head against a stone on the ground. Bopoluchi took the pestle and pounded the witch's head with all her might, killing her with a single blow.

It was a horrible thing, to be sure, and Bopoluchi held her hands to her face for an unending moment as she contemplated the murder she had just committed. But such a deed was preferable, she convinced herself, to a life of slavery. She knew that the robber would be returning soon, and forced herself out of her reverie. She then dressed the crone in the wedding dress, propped her up in a chair, and covered the crone's face with the veil.

Bopoluchi then collected all the gold and jewels that the robber had stashed in the hovel and escaped into the woods. By sheer luck, she found the main path, and located the carriage tracks that indicated the direction of the village. With all her youthful vigour, she ran back to her father's house.

When the robber returned to his hovel, he was carrying a large spinning wheel for his new wife to work on. When he saw her sitting in her wedding dress, he called out to her. Of course, there was no answer, so he called again. Once more there was no answer. Being a violent short-tempered man, he threw the spinning wheel at the veiled figure, knocking it down. It was surely his intent to kill Bopoluchi, thinking, perhaps, that he could always steal for himself another bride.

When he discovered that the veiled figure was not Bopoluchi, after all, but his own mother, he cried in despair, for he believed that he had killed her. Quite unlike his regular self, he felt true guilt for the first time in his life. He was so racked with this guilt that he left the area for good, unwilling to remain near the site of his most horrid crime.

To say that Bopoluchi's father was glad to see her would be an understatement indeed. The old man had missed his daughter dearly, and would rather have lived in destitution with his child than to have spent another hour without her. So he was quite relieved to have her back, more so for the horrible tale of her abduction that she then related to him.

The jewels that the girl had taken from the robber's hovel were indeed tempting, but they knew what they must do. Bopoluchi and her father gave back to the other villagers all of the jewels that had been stolen from them. Surprisingly, there was still considerable wealth left over from the robber's stash.

They were now very wealthy people indeed, and knew that everything would be all right.

THE BULBUL

There once was a young girl whom we shall call Manjula. Like all young girls, Manjula wanted to play. Her favourite distractions involved flowers and insects, rounded meadows and glistening brooks. She would run along the water, chasing dragonflies and picking blossoms, inventing fanciful adventures and scenarios within her mind.

But time did not always allow her to play. For four hours every day, like many children her age, Manjula had to go to school. The schoolhouse was not a pleasurable place, at least not as pleasurable as the meadows and brooks. It was true that many of her friends were there, but that was not enough to compensate for the stacks of reading and arithmetic that the schoolmistress required of her.

She once asked her mother why she had to spend so much time in school. Her mother had told her that, without an education, she would be unable to get a job when she grew up, and would also be less able to attract a worthy husband. Manjula pouted at this answer, and wished most strenuously that she didn't have to go to school ever again, and that she were as rich as a princess without the need of a job or husband.

A *bulbul*, a little brown bird, watched the girl make her wish, and took it upon himself to show her the errors of her desires. He swooped down upon her and lifted her up into his wings. She was so tiny a child that the *bulbul* could easily fly with her added weight.

Manjula was frightened at first, but was much too excited by the fanciful flight to be dismayed by her predicament. So high in the air, she could see much of the land, and could make out the people as if they were the insects with which she loved to play.

The bird carried her far across the meadows to a neighbouring village where poverty was quite prevalent. He settled upon a thatched roof where, below, another young girl toiled at her chores. The two watchers heard the new girl talking to herself: "I wish I could go to school," the girl said. "If only my family didn't need me here, I could go to school like all the other young girls."

The *bulbul* swept up again, but this time flew his passenger further north across the great river. They settled upon the balustrade of the king's palace. From there, he and Manjula could see yet another little girl --a princess!-- moping about the courtyard.

"I wish I weren't the king's daughter," the princess said to herself. "If we weren't so rich, I could play outside the palace walls like the other little girls."

At that, the *bulbul* swept up one last time, and returned his passenger to the familiar garden of her mother's house. The lesson that Manjula had learned that day was an obvious one, and she never again desired to be anything or anyone other than who she was.

THE KING OF CHEATS

In one of the eastern provinces there lived a man who was renowned throughout the village as a great cheat. It was said that he could swindle the hairs off of a man's head, his skill was so great. But with great skill, and with no one in the small village to contest his ability, he soon grew arrogant. He became convinced that he was indeed the king of all cheats.

One day, he was compelled to visit the city to make some deliveries. Upon his back, he carried a bag of ashes to be dumped by the river. Soon, he came upon a local city-dweller who was also carrying a bag upon his back. "Brother," he called out to the local man. "What is in your sac?"

"Fresh mangoes!" the city man answered back. "What are you carrying?"

"Spices," lied the village cheat. "I've grown too much this season. What say I trade my sac for yours?"

The city man's eyes lit up, for indeed spices were more valuable than mangoes any day. He agreed to the exchange, and both men sped off with the other's sac without checking the contents first.

When the village cheat reached his home, he could not restrain his jubilance at having swindled a city man; he was near bursting with self satisfaction.

"Listen!" he called to his wife, "today I traded a sac of ashes for a sac of mangoes..." But, as he emptied the sac, all he found were ashes!

"You've been swindled by a city cheat!" his wife laughed, pleased that her arrogant husband had received his comeuppance. Sure enough, miles away, the city cheat was facing a similar derision from his wife for having traded a sac of ashes for yet another sac of ashes.

Some days passed, and once more the village cheat found that he had business in the city. As India is a land of fate and irony, it was not surprising that once again he came upon the city cheat. The two of them eyed each other suspiciously --resentfully but respectfully. After some time, their commonality won out, and the two became fast friends.

"Brother," said one to the other. "Let us vow never to cheat each other again."

"Agreed," said the other. "With the two of us together, no city or town is safe!" They laughed together and immediately sped off to a neighbouring town, intent on combining their deceptive talents for greater financial gain.

Once in their new arena, they took to their task with glee, essentially stealing from every merchant or passerby they encountered, using a variety of old but proven schemes. Eventually, they came to an old woman's home. They endeavoured to swindle this unsuspecting woman with one of their practiced routines.

"Madam," they said to her, "You probably don't remember us, but we are distant relatives of yours. We have come to invite you to our niece's wedding several days hence."

The old woman was of course delighted, and much abashed at not remembering her kinsfolk. To make amends, she invited the two to stay the night.

That evening, the cheats stole a golden cup from the old woman's shelf, and told her the next morning that a crow had flown in and taken it when the window was open. The simple and trusting woman believed the cheats, though was saddened for her loss.

As it happened, the theft was witnessed by the old woman's youngest servant, Ravi "the Fly", so named for his diminutive form and protruding shoulder blades. Ravi had been sitting in the shadows of the pantry when the two cheats had rifled through the shelves, but they had failed to notice the boy for his smallness and darkness.

Ravi said nothing to the old woman, though, for a servant would have such little cachet with his employer against her supposed kinsmen. However, the old woman ordered Ravi the Fly to guide the two cheats back to the main road lest they fall prey to brigands on their way home. Ravi went happily.

"Listen," Ravi told the two men as they walked along the main road. "I know this way well. The people here have strange customs, and it would take me a long time to explain them to you. All you need to know is that whenever someone asks you, 'one or two', you must always answer 'two.' Do you understand?"

The two cheats indicated that they did indeed understand, and were grateful for Ravi's guidance. Soon, they came upon a large fortified house with many servants and guardsmen. Ravi indicated that they needed to stop here for a while. A burly man came out to speak with Ravi, then turned to the two cheats. He asked, "one or two?"

Instantly, the two cheats countered, "Two!"

The burly man turned to Ravi and said, "Two slaves for sale? Excellent!" He handed Ravi a bag of money and motioned for his guards to take the cheats in tow. The two men objected fiercely, of course, but to no avail.

Smirking to himself, Ravi headed back into the town from which they had just departed. Now armed with riches, he didn't need to be a servant anymore. He stopped by a food stand staffed by a young boy, and started to eat all of the sweets!

"Hey!" said the boy, "you must pay for those!"

"I'm a friend of your father," Ravi replied, still eating. "My name is 'the Fly'. Go run and tell him."

The little boy ran to find his father and told him, "The fly is eating all the food!" To which the father responded, "And how much food can one fly eat? Never mind the fly, idiot, and get back to the food stand!"

By the time the boy had returned, Ravi had fled with his stomach sated. In his rush, he didn't notice a large lumbering figure lurking in his periphery. It was a wild bear! The bear knocked Ravi to the ground and began tearing at his clothes. His bag of money tore apart, and the bear's snout was covered with bills of currency.

A wandering merchant came upon this scene, and was struck by the vision of a bear from whose snout money seemed to flow! He helped Ravi beat the bear into submission, but had to ask about the money.

"Ah, it's a curse," Ravi said. "This bear produces money out of its snout. But then it gets restless, and I have to wrestle with it."

"I don't mind wrestling," said the merchant, his greed triggered by Ravi's words. "What say I buy this bear from you?"

"Well," said Ravi. "Since his snout is my main source of income, I couldn't part with it for less than one thousand!"

"Done!" And Ravi walked away from the scene suddenly an immensely wealthy man.

It was about this time that the city cheat and the village cheat finally managed to convince the burly slaver that they had been tricked into being sold. They had made a small fortune during their swindling escapades these past days, so were able to buy their freedom. They immediately headed back into town to find Ravi.

They found instead the old woman whose golden cup they had stolen. She had finally put things together in her mind, and was aware of their criminality. They had no choice but to return her gold... with interest.

Following Ravi's trail, they came upon the food stand that the Fly had robbed. The father had his stupid's son by the ear, and was busily scolding him for having allowed Ravi to steal so much food.

The two cheats began to describe Ravi to them, wishing to find out where he had gone. Thinking them to be Ravi's associates, the food stand's owner forced the cheats to compensate him for his loss. Despite their protests, the two had no choice but to capitulate; they were rapidly running out of money.

Then they came upon the travelling merchant with his worthless bear. The merchant was furious, of course, since the bear was unable to produce money from its snout. His rage was so violent and threatening that the cheats had no choice but to pay him the money that Ravi had swindled.

Eventually, after much time, cost and toil, they found Ravi asleep under a coconut tree. They debated in hushed whispers what course to take.

"We should kill him!" the city cheat said.

"No, Brother! We are not killers! We should sell *him* into slavery and recoup our losses!" They bickered thus for some time, but reached no consensus. Admitting that this was beyond their league, the cheats summoned the local authorities and had Ravi arrested for his crimes. Best let the law handle the likes of Ravi the Fly. Indeed, they looked forward to bearing witness against him at Ravi's official trial.

Oddly, Ravi was silent when they put him in jail, charged with a variety of crimes. He was saving his strength for thinking, it seemed, for his devious mind was set to work devising a way to free himself.

Finally, while awaiting his trial, Ravi struck upon an idea. He scribbled a royal decree upon some parchment, and managed to throw it from his jail cell to the sentry's feet. It read: "By order of the king: until further notice, all foreigners to this city must leave by nightfall or be executed as spies."

As was required of him, the sentry went straight to the courtyard and read the decree aloud for all the townsfolk to hear. Upon hearing it, the two cheats were terrified. They were not from this town, after all, and so could easily be mistaken for spies. They immediately fled for their homes far away from the town.

So abashed they were that they vowed never again to swindle others.

With the absence of prime witnesses and accusers, Ravi easily won his trial and was set free.

Later on, once well away from the cursed town, the former village cheat said to the former city cheat, " You know what? I think Ravi the Fly was indeed the king of cheats."

TWO DEAF MEN

An old man who was hard of hearing was in a foul mood. After having quarrelled with his wife over some minor household point, he stormed out of the house and squatted by the side of the road, waiting for his anger to subside.

A shepherd came by then, desperately searching for his lost cow and calf. It so happened, oddly enough, that the shepherd was nearly deaf, too. The shepherd saw the old man, and took note of his sternness, concluding that this must be a wise man indeed, for only the wisest of men could be of such foul disposition brought about by serious contemplation of the world's woes.

"O wise man," the shepherd said. "Can you tell me where my lost cow and calf have gone?" The old man could not hear the shepherd, of course, so merely ignored him.

The shepherd tried harder, with more gesturing. "Please tell me where my animals are. I promise that if you help me find them, I will let you have the calf!" The old man was furious now, and pointed his finger at the shepherd, hurling insults at him.

Of course, the deaf shepherd could not hear the old man, but took his pointing to be an indication of where the cow and calf had gone. He thanked the old man and quickly went on his way.

By sheer luck alone, the shepherd found his lost animals. Along the way, however, the calf had suffered a minor accident; its tail was broken. True to his word, however, he returned to give the calf to the old man.

"O wise man," the shepherd said. "Here is your reward for having given me such good advice. Many thanks."

The old man mistook these words to mean that he was to blame for the calf's broken tail. "I will not pay for your injured calf!" he exclaimed, and rudely shoved the animal back to the shepherd.

The shepherd, in turn, thought that the old man was demanding not the calf, but the cow as a reward. "Greedy man!" he intoned, "You will not have my cow! Take the calf and be done with it!"

This exchange continued for some minutes until a disreputable young man happened by. He quickly understood what was happening, and shouted into the shepherd's ear: "Leave the calf with me. I will make him take it!"

The shepherd agreed, and went off with his cow in tow. The young man then bent close to the remaining deaf man and shouted in his ear: "Don't worry about the calf. I will tend to its broken tail!"

The old man returned to his home, neither he nor the shepherd ever realizing that they had been swindled.

THE DEBT

It was the way of the people of certain parts of the country that debts of the fathers are borne by the sons. Thus, subsequent generations are accountable for loans offered to an ancestor.

Chowdhuri was a hard-working farmer who had a problem. His great-grandfather had, a century ago, taken out a loan from the local money-lender, the *mahajan*, for the sum of one hundred rupees. The interest had compounded so much over the years that Chowdhuri, through no fault of his own, now owed one thousand rupees --a sum far in excess of the total value of his lands.

On one particular afternoon, he was taking his monthly walk to the present *mahajan*'s domicile to pay the regular installment of the ancient debt. On the way, he bumped into Madhuri, a prosperous merchant whose clever and devious ways had made him relatively wealthy.

"Where are you off to, Chowdhuri?" Madhuri the merchant called.

"To pay part of my loan to the *mahajan*," Chowdhuri sighed. "At the rate that the interest is accruing, I will soon be unable to pay, and all my property may be forfeit."

"Let me walk with you, friend," Madhuri said. "I have business with the *mahajan*, too."

As they walked, Madhuri became bored with the farmer's gloomy disposition. "Listen, friend," he said. "Let's tell each other stories, eh? Why be upset with your loan. You can't do anything about it. Best put your mind elsewhere."

"That's true," Chowdhuri agreed. "Let's tell each other the most outrageous stories we can think of!" He brightened.

"All right," agreed Madhuri the merchant. "But," he added deviously, "let neither of us claim the other is lying --no matter how outrageous the tale he tells!"

"Good idea," Chowdhuri said, intrigued. "If any one of us denies the story of the other, he must pay him one thousand rupees!"

Madhuri laughed at this, sure that the farmer would slip up along the way. Local observers agreed that this was a fair stipulation, and it was they way of such men to take these kinds of wagers very seriously, especially when witnesses are present.

As they walked, the merchant volunteered to begin. "Have I ever told you about my great-grandfather?" he asked.

"No, Madhuri, you haven't."

"Well, Chowdhuri, he was a poor farmer just like you. He toiled on the lands until he lost his labouring job one season. So he went to the city where he found a talking snake."

"Of course, Madhuri," Chowdhuri agreed, suppressing a grin, not wishing to break the rules.

"Yes," Madhuri continued. "The talking snake told my ancestor to jump into the river and to seek out the aquatic people, which he did."

"Of course, Madhuri."

"The aquatic people instructed my ancestor in the arts of animal mind control. When he returned to the surface, he sought out the king's caravan. When he saw the king's elephant, he used his mind control powers to cause the elephant to rear back on his hind legs."

"Of course, Madhuri. That is most certainly true," Chowdhuri said.

"Well, once the elephant was thus reared, my great-grandfather rushed forward and rescued the king from the beast's back. The king was so grateful that he made my ancestor the first minister of the kingdom!"

"Indeed, Madhuri, that is most true." Chowdhuri struggled to conceal the incredulity from his gravelly voice.

Madhuri continued: "My ancestor served the king well for many years, accruing such a huge fortune that he singlehandedly purchased the entire country of Punjab!"

"Yes, Madhuri, most certainly."

Madhuri beamed with satisfaction, fully enjoying this opportunity to tell grand unapologetic lies. "My own father, growing up in such an environment, naturally became the king's ambassador to China. He learned such great foreign arts from that country, that, when he returned, his head was twice the size of his body, and it had to be carted before him upon a high chariot."

"Indeed, Madhuri, indeed."

"The bulk of my family's fortune passed to my eldest brother. All that was left to me was my business. But I also have vast tracts of property in the kingdom of the aquatic people. But since I cannot hold my breath for very long, it is a meaningless possession."

"Very true, Madhuri," Chowdhuri agreed. "May I tell my story now?"

Madhuri agreed, so the farmer began his own outrageous

tale: "My own great-grandfather had superhuman strength. Nightly, he would heave the entire kingdom upon his head and carry it about the coastline. In that way, all the farm lands enjoyed good sea air and plentiful sunlight."

Madhuri almost laughed aloud at the blatant and colourful lie, but remembered the rules of the game: "Of course, Chowdhuri, of course."

"Well, Madhuri, remember how your great-grandfather was originally a poor farm labourer? Well, he used to labour for *my* great-grandfather!" Madhuri didn't like the sounds of where this was going, but played along by uttering, "true, true."

At this point, the duo arrived at the *mahajan*'s domicile. The old money-lender greeted them kindly, but the two men ignored him, they were so caught up in their storytelling. Chowdhuri continued: "As you mentioned, your great-grandfather fell upon poor times, so was forced to leave the farm to seek his fortunes elsewhere."

"True, Chowdhuri, true."

"My own ancestor was so concerned with your great-grandfather's plight that he loaned him one hundred rupees."

"True, Chowdhuri, true," Madhuri said, hesitatingly.

"Well," Chowdhuri said, "with accrued interest, that debt now comes to one thousand rupees, which you now owe to me..."

"Um...true..."

Chowdhuri had him. "You have admitted the debt before a witness, the *mahajan*, so I now ask that you pay *him* the money that you owe me, thus clearing my own debt in full."

Madhuri was livid at having been thus tricked. But he had indeed admitted the debt before a witness, and if he now claimed that Chowdhuri had lied, must himself pay one thousand rupees in penalty. Being a wealthy man, he easily afforded the price, so reluctantly paid it. But Madhuri never again underestimated the farmers of the land, and viewed them all with hesitant respect and distrust.

It was some months later that Madhuri went to the *mahajan* to take out a loan for a new business venture. "If you have trouble paying," the *mahajan* said innocently, "you can always sell some of that land you have with the aquatic people."

THE DEMON AND THE THIEF

There was once a thief who was intent on stealing the only two cows of a lowly farmer. While it is indeed a very cruel thing to steal from one who is so poor, this thief suffered from a great paucity of compassion and of good nature. He had been watching this particular farmer for several days, and his desire had long ago quashed any goodness within him.

One moonless night, he began to execute his plan. He crept slowly and devilishly across the meadow until he was within striking distance of the farmer's home. There, much to his surprise, he beheld a hideous unearthly sight. Lurking about the hut was yellow-skinned, goat-footed creature with the eyes and hands of a man, but the horns of a bull and the tongue of a snake.

The thief was without fear, however, since evil shall never have fear of evil. "What are you?" he asked the vile thing, careful to keep his voice beneath a whisper.

"I am a demon, man. I've come to eat this farmer as he sleeps."

"Well, I'm a thief, and I've come to take his two cows. So, wait a few moments until I have the cows, then you can eat him."

"But no!" hissed the demon. "If you make a noise and wake him, I may not be able to eat him! I must eat first, then you may take the cows."

The thief became angry. "Look. What if he's able to say a prayer when you try to eat him? Then you'll have been banished, and he'll be awake. Then how can I steal the cows?"

"You will wait for me!" the demon hissed.

"No!" the thief shouted. "You will wait for me."

With all this noise, the farmer woke up with a start. The demon turned to the farmer and said, "O pious farmer, this thief is here to steal your cows! It is a good thing that I caught him for you!"

"Brother," the thief protested. "Don't believe him. Look at this vile creature, so hideous and foul. This demon is here to devour you! I've come to beat him off."

The farmer never hesitated. He said a quick prayer to his god, and the demon vanished in a puff of smoke, never to return. The farmer then grabbed the club he kept near his hammock, and beat the thief savagely, forcing him to run away in agony.

No one bothered that farmer --or his cows-- ever again.

DIMNAH AND SHANZIBAH

One day, while being led through the forest by his master, a huge bull named Shanzibah fell into a deep crevice. When his master could not find him, he assumed Shanzibah was lost forever. The bull was so distraught that he bellowed a sad but terrible wail that echoed through the forest.

The king of the forest, the Lion, heard this awful sound and was stricken with terror. Whatever magnificent and fierce beast that issued such a sound must also be powerful enough to defeat in combat any animal, even the Lion! Overcome with this anxiety, the sovereign cat retreated to his lair and surrounded himself with courtiers, refusing to leave the safety of his demesnes.

Word of the Lion's seclusion spread quickly throughout the forest, and was a source of mystery, gossip and concern. The security of any realm is often dependent upon the courage of its leader, after all, so anxieties began to deepen throughout the animal kingdom.

Dimnah the jackal was one who became thus concerned. "Perhaps," he said to his thoughtful friend Kalilah, another jackal, "I should offer my services as an advisor to the Lion."

"Foolish, very foolish," Kalilah said disapprovingly. "There are three things every wise person should avoid doing. The first is to taste poison to see what it is; the second is to tell secrets to untrustworthy individuals; and the third is to become involved in the affairs of the King. No good will come of this, Dimnah."

"Very true, friend," Dimnah agreed. "But one must also seek to rise in one's station in life. Great strides can only be accomplished through great risk. It takes courage to do three things, Kalilah: to face your enemies, to undertake business at a distance, and to become involved in the King's affairs. As I am both wise and courageous, I shall endeavour to do the last."

Kalilah contemplated these words, and admitted that there was truth in them. "But how will you become an advisor to the Lion King?"

"Every advisor rises to that station by demonstrating his wisdom. The King is troubled now. I will discover the reason for his unhappiness, and will seek to alleviate it. Through my honesty and helpfulness, he will come to understand that my counsel is invaluable."

Kalilah could find no flaw in his friend's reasoning, so merely raised his eyebrows and slitted his eyelids in further contemplation.

Dimnah, meanwhile, brought his plan into action. He went to the Lion's demesnes and requested an audience. When he was finally allowed to speak to the King, he said, "Majesty, why have you sequestered yourself here?"

The King was surprisingly candid. "Because, jackal, I have heard the most terrible sound in the forest. Surely it is the roar of a greater beast than I."

Upon hearing these words, the King's counsellors protested theatrically: "No, Sire! You are the mightiest of beasts! There can be no other!"

But Dimnah was calm and refused to act the sycophant. "Sire, if this beast is truly more powerful than you, then you truly have cause to worry. What if I find him, and bring him here so that he, too, might be your subject? Would that not assure you of your superiority over him?"

"You would do this for me, jackal?" The Lion asked. In response, Dimnah bowed deeply. "If you succeed, Dimnah," the Lion continued, "I will make you my closest advisor."

Dimnah smiled knowingly and set out into the forest to complete his mission.

Presently, he, too, heard the braying of the bull. Quelling his natural fear by calling upon his reason, Dimnah followed the bellows to the crevice that had trapped the desperate bull.

"Ahoy!" he called to Shanzibah, the trapped bull.

"Help me!" Shanzibah cried back. Dimnah saw the bull for the first time then, and was admittedly impressed by Shanzibah's girth, toughness, ferocity and musculature.

"If I help you to freedom," Dimnah replied, "will you promise to pledge allegiance to the Lion King, and vow to be his subject until your death?"

"I will promise!" Shanzibah replied unhesitatingly.

After some contemplation, Dimnah reasoned out how he should free the big bull. With his forepaws, he dug away at the shallow lip of the crevice until a way was opened for Shanzibah to walk out. True to his word, Shanzibah followed Dimnah to the Lion's court.

When the bull heaved his immense form before the pampered courtiers, they cowered in terror, some even dropping to their knees in toadying appeasement of Shanzibah's obvious strength. The Lion himself was duly impressed and frightened, but refused to slink from his throne.

"Your Majesty," Dimnah said, "may I present Shanzibah the

bull, your servant."

When Shanzibah bowed deeply before his new master, the courtiers both cheered and sighed in relief.

The Lion was duly pleased, and immediately raised Dimnah to the rank of Chief Advisor. Dimnah, it seemed, had proven that honesty, courage and efficiency could indeed ensure one's professional success.

In the coming months, Shanzibah proved to be an excellent subject, having been primed for this from his tenure as a bonded farm animal. He worked hard to please the Lion, and was naturally honest and earnest. As they grew closer, Shanzibah was able to offer the Lion counsel on a number of stately matters. nd in due time, the Lion decreed that Shanzibah would replace Dimnah as Chief Advisor.

Dejected, Dimnah returned to Kalilah and conceded, "Honour is due, my friend. You were right, and I was wrong."

Kalilah nodded his acknowledgement. But he added, "Consider what has trespassed, Dimnah. The king was frightened, which would not do for a safe a stable kingdom. A beast was trapped. And an intellect, trapped in the body of a well-muscled bull, had gone to waste. Now none of those things are true. The kingdom is happy, the king is content, a beast suffers no more, and a proper advisor now serves our monarch. All of this came to pass because you, Dimnah, sought to do, rather than merely to contemplate.

"Honour is due you, my friend."

THE FALL OF DIMNAH

As the months passed, Dimnah the jackal discovered that he could not be content with having his position as First Minister usurped by Shanzibah the Bull. He turned to his friend Kalilah for guidance.

Kalilah chastised him. "You sought personal advancement, and received it through honour. We are all better for your actions. Why now do you seek to dishonour a colleague? What good can come of this?"

"Shanzibah enjoys his position because of my good service to the lion king, true?" Dimnah asked.

"Yes, that is true."

"Then surely I should benefit from his success, as well?"

"Your logic is flawed, Dimnah." Kalilah offered.

"Perhaps," Dimnah continued. "But I will nonetheless seek the downfall of Shanzibah."

"And how will that further your career?" Kalilah demanded.

"It will not, friend. But in removing Shanzibah from the court, I will in effect be serving the king. And because my motivation is thus pure, I am sure to succeed."

Kalilah was not convinced of his fellow's conviction. Surely this was a rationalization for seeking vengeance upon poor innocent Shanzibah. "And how, Dimnah, does your plan serve the king or the realm?"

Dimnah paused to consider his words. Then spoke: "It is clear, Kalilah, that Shanzibah is enjoying great favour and power at court. There can be but one king, and so Shanzibah's power denudes that of the true king."

"Dimnah," Kalilah said, departing, "both your wisdom and your goodness are sadly in short supply today. No good will come of this."

Thus, Dimnah set out to seek another audience with the lion, his former employer. He trekked across the forest to the lion's demesnes, and requested a private word with the king. Because of his former station within the court, he was granted this small request.

"Sire," Dimnah said, "I come to you as a loyal servant. I have been hearing rumours that are most disturbing. There are whispers that Shanzibah your minister is plotting against you. He has been gathering support amongst the troops, declaring you to be old and soft."

At this, the king bristled. True, he was aging, but was still a terrible and ferocious predator. What was more disturbing was this poor characterization of his trusted friend Shanzibah. "Surely, Dimnah, this cannot be true!"

"I cannot believe it either, sire."

"Then I will order Shanzibah to leave the kingdom and never to return."

"I'm sorry, sire, but that will not be enough. Once gone from the forest, Shanzibah will surely gather support and come back with force. A traitor and conspirator cannot be tolerated to persist."

"What then should I do? I cannot kill him without more proof of his wrongdoing."

"Well," Dimnah said slyly, "why not invite him to an audience? If he looks about hesitatingly, it will be clear that he has been plotting against you. Then you may kill him."

The lion thought for a few moments, then reluctantly agreed that this was an acceptable plan.

Dimnah sped from the king's court to visit minister Shanzibah. The bull was pleased to see the jackal, and remembered well their good times together. He made to embrace Dimnah. But Dimnah interrupted: "Shanzibah! I haven't much time!"

"What is it, Dimnah?"

"I've just come from the king. He is jealous of your popularity, and fears that you may usurp his throne. When he summons you later, he will have his archers shoot you from either side!"

Shanzibah was both angered and afraid. Sure enough, word came for him to attend an audience with the king, and he dutifully obeyed. He heaved his immense form toward the royal demesnes and entered cautiously. Remembering Dimnah's words, he cast his gaze to the left and right, searching out the hidden archers.

When the lion king saw the bull's sideways glances, he remembered Dimnah's advice and concluded, erroneously, that Shanzibah was plotting. Enraged, the king leapt from his throne and sank his teeth into Shanzibah's neck. In time, the bull died with a terrible shudder.

There was much mourning in the kingdom, for Shanzibah's goodness and service were well known. Even the king wept openly, doubting at last the veracity of Dimnah's claims.

Such treachery could not remain hidden indefinitely, and gradually word came that Shanzibah was indeed innocent, and that Dimnah had plotted his death.

So Dimnah, too, was sentenced to imprisonment and death for his betrayal.

In the end, Kalilah declared to all, "this, then, is the result of lying, and of being unfair to others. Dimnah was among the wisest of us all. But even the wise can fall prey to vanity and ambition."

THE DREAMERS

There once was a young couple who spent most of their time daydreaming. On a particular lazy afternoon, as they lounged about in their bungalow, the husband said aloud, "One day, when I have enough money, I'm going to buy a cow."

"Mmmm, yes," said the wife. "And when you get that cow, I will milk it every day."

The husband was pleased with this, but frowned. "If you're going to milk our cow so frequently," he said, "you're going to need some bigger pots to keep the milk in."

"You're right!" the wife said, concerned. "I'll need three new pots --one for milk, and one for cream."

"What about the third pot?"

"Oh," said the wife. "The third pot is for my sister. I'll give some milk to her every day."

The husband was enraged. He leapt to his feet, found a stick and began to beat his wife with it. "You ungrateful woman!" he cried. "I work so hard to buy us a cow, and you go and give a third of our milk to your worthless sister!"

The wife was headstrong, too. She found her own stick, and beat her husband harder. "You ungrateful man!" she shouted. "I toil every day milking our cow. This is how you reward me?!"

A neighbour had been listening to this sorry exchange, and decided to drop by just then. He brought his own stick, and proceeded to beat both the husband and the wife.

"Hey!" the husband protested. "Why are you beating us?"

"That's for my vegetable garden!" the neighbour said.

"But," the wife pointed out, "You don't have a vegetable garden."

"Not yet," the neighbour replied. "But I've been thinking about growing one. And when I do, your sorry cow will surely trample all over it!"

THE LUCKY SHEPHERD

There once was a powerful and vain king who was convinced that no one could guess his thoughts or rival his intellect. He challenged his minister to bring to the court someone who could match his regal wits.

The minister was very eager to find such a clever person, if only to help quell the king's growing vanity. After a thorough search, however, the minister could find no one clever enough to match the king. "As I predicted," the king said, "there is no one worthy to test my intellect."

The minister bristled. In desperation and anger, he grabbed the first man he saw outside the palace --a poor shepherd-- and brought him to the royal court. "This man," the minister declared, "will satisfy any test of intelligence you can offer."

The shepherd was confused and a bit frightened, of course, but stood there nonetheless, silently awaiting the king's test. The king studied the man for a while, sizing him up, perhaps assessing his bearing and skull size. Eventually, the monarch held up one finger.

Silently, but assuredly, the shepherd held up two fingers in response.

The king was impressed, but said nothing. Instead, he held up three fingers. At this, the shepherd shook his head and turned to leave.

The king laughed aloud and rushed to prevent the shepherd from leaving.

"This indeed is a man as clever as me," the king proclaimed. "When I held up one finger, I was asking if I am the most powerful person here. But this man held up two fingers, reminding me that there is also God."

The minister raised an eyebrow, but said nothing. The king continued: "And when I held up three fingers, I was asking him whether there could be a third powerful person. Rightly, he refused to accept that possibility, and turned his back to me."

The king was immensely pleased and clapped both the shepherd and the minister on the back. "I am no longer alone in my genius, and I have you both to thank." He then rewarded them both with bags of gold, and retired to his rooms.

As the shepherd was escorted out of the palace, the minister asked him: "I'm curious. How were you able to understand the king?"

"Actually, sir," the shepherd said, somewhat apologetically. "When the king held up one finger, I thought he was asking for one of my three sheep. He is the king, after all, so I offered two instead. When he held up three fingers, I thought he wanted all three of my sheep! I thought that this was being greedy indeed, so I shook my head and tried to run away!"

At this, the minister had a good laugh, and handed the shepherd an extra bag of gold.

THE HARE OF
THE MOON

During a particularly dry season, a tribe of elephants found their water supply short. Being elephants, and therefore used to having their own way, they chose to take over another pond, rather than to practice frugality and conservation. These elephants, after all, were powerful, but none too bright.

The nearest pond, it so happened, was inhabited by a tribe of hares. Of course, the hares could not offer any kind of resistance to the bullying elephants, and so were immediately dispersed into the forest, their precious pond overtaken and abused by the brutish pachyderms.

The hares were desperate to get their pond back, and sought help from the eldest of their number, an ancient hare named Vijaya.

"Don't despair," Vijaya said. "I'll get rid of the elephants, and we'll have our pond back."

That very night, Vijaya approached the reclining elephants. It must have been an impressive sight: an entire herd of enormous creatures frolicking in the moonlight, dwarfing everything around them, glorying in vain opulent muscularity. But Vijaya seemed unafraid.

The elephants were not startled by Vijaya's appearance, but did watch him distrustfully. "Who are you, silly hare?" the chief elephant demanded.

"I am Vijaya," said the little rodent, "ambassador of the Hares of the Moon."

"And what is your business?"

"I have come on behalf of my lord to demand that our pond be returned to us." Vijaya spoke with assuredness, never wavering from his task, even though the elephants swaggered about him, beaming glares of aggressive intent.

"How dare you!" the chief elephant exclaimed. "What power do the Hares of the Moon possess that they can hope to sway us elephants, the most powerful beasts of the forest?"

Vijaya smiled sagely. "We are nothing more than small and weak hares. But our master and protector is greater than your entire tribe combined. He is brilliant and enormous, and hovers above you at this moment. Our master is none other than the Moon himself!"

The chief elephant roared a deafening laugh. "That's a good story, hare. But what proof do you have that you serve the Moon?"

"Come," Vijaya said. He led the elephants to the pond and bade them look into it. "See? Our Master deigns to allow his reflection to appear in our pond. He protects us."

The elephants were stunned. One by one, they apologized to Vijaya and shuffled back into the forest, cowed by their fear of the Moon.

The hares reclaimed their pond, and were never bothered again.

HARISHARAM THE FROG

There once was a particularly foolish young man named Harisharam who, in his youth, was called The Frog for his stout appearance. Indeed, his head was big and wide, and his mouth stretched from ear to ear, much like a real frog. In adulthood, Harisharam still referred to himself as "Frog," and that his how his wife and closest friends knew him.

Harisharam the Frog was desperate for people to take him seriously. You see, because of his odd appearance and his annoying habit of talking to himself aloud, he was not well regarded in the community.

Now, it was known that a local land owner named Stuladatta was holding a wedding for his daughter. It was customary in this time that the bridegroom be given a horse to ride during the marriage ceremony, and Stuladatta had procured a fine and expensive horse for his daughter's special day.

Seizing upon an idea to raise his status in the community, Harisharam waited until the night before the wedding, and stole the horse and tied it to a large tree at the edge of the forest. He then instructed his wife to tell Stuladatta that Harisharam the Frog was in fact a master astrologer who could locate the horse.

Harisharam's wife didn't care much for her husband's trickery, feeling that it demeaned them both. She warned him, "No good will come of this, Frog. Sometimes I wonder why I married you."

But she went along with the silly plan, perhaps secretly savouring the opportunity to interact with the locale elite. When she went to Stuladatta's house, she discovered a household in disarray and panic. The disappearance of the horse had indeed wrought its desired effect.

The wife delivered the message, restraining her own laughter while expressing the potency of her husband's astrological powers. Sure enough, Stuladatta sent for Harisharam to divine the whereabouts of the missing horse.

Understanding the importance of theatre, Harisharam made his entrance a dramatic one, with much pomp and flourish. Before Stuladatta and his household, Harisharam uttered some gibberish, made meaningless gestures, then gave the location of the horse as if he had extracted it from the stars:

"You will find the horse," he spoke mystically, "tied to a large tree at the near edge of the forest." When Stuladatta sent his men out to look, they found the horse just where Harisharam had left it.

Everyone believed that Harisharam was indeed the wise astrologer he claimed to be, and the Frog enjoyed a new heightened station in the eyes of his peers. He dined with Stuladatta regularly now, and even his doubting wife was enjoying many of the social perks of their new status. As the weeks progressed, his reputation grew, and soon he was one of the most respected men in the region outside the village.

Some time later, the king's jewels were stolen from the palace, and the royal ministers were unable to discover their whereabouts. Royal soldiers were sent to the far corners of the province to question peasants and travellers, yet no sign was found of the treasure. Harisharam's reputation had grown so large via the kingdom's rabid gossip network that even the king's ministers had heard of him. In desperation, the king sent for Harisharam the Frog, the story of the wedding horse having reached his royal ears.

Harisharam was escorted to the palace, a bit cowed by the power and regalness of the king's demesnes. Stuladatta's house had been fine and large, but the royal palace grounds were a realm of such size and opulence that Harisharam's theatrical heart was hard pressed to confer upon him the dignity to which he had become accustomed in recent weeks.

It was all he could do to keep from trembling with fear.

"Harisharam," the king said. "If you can tell me where my jewels are, I will reward you handsomely!"

Harisharam was petrified, of course. He had no idea who had stolen the jewels, and was sure the king would discover his deceit. His first impulse was to admit that he was a fake, as his wife had demanded he do. But he realized that his community would ostracize him, and he would be forced to flee in shame. Perhaps it was best to leave the kingdom for good, before his fakery were discovered.

He bought himself some time. "I will need an evening to meditate, O king. I will give you my answer in the morning."

He had intended to use the evening to gather his wife and belongings, and to steal far away during the night. But the king surprised him, insisting that Harisharam spend his night of meditation locked within the royal palace.

Distraught, Harisharam was then escorted to his room.

Now, it so happened that the jewels had been stolen by one of the palace maids, a woman named Jivha whose gossipy ways had earned her the nickname of "The Tongue." Jivha the Tongue had heard of Harisharam's skills, and was nervous that he would be able to sense her guilt. So, she placed her ear to his bedroom door in hopes of hearing his meditations.

What she heard was Harisharam cursing himself and fretting about the morning. He was sure that his own loose tongue had taken him to this dire situation.

"O tongue," Harisharam said to himself, "why have you brought me to this sorry predicament!" On hearing this, the maid was convinced that Harisharam had been addressing her. She burst into his room and dropped to Harisharam's feet.

"O, kind sir," she pleaded. "Please forgive me for stealing the jewels! What can I do to escape punishment?"

Harisharam was stunned, of course, but recovered quickly. His natural crafty ways took over. "You must tell me the exact location of where you have hidden the jewels," he answered. "If you do so, I promise not to give you up to the king."

Jivha agreed, and Harisharam was told that the jewels were in fact hidden beneath a large boulder on the beach.

The next morning, Harisharam was called to the king's court. There, he performed the mandatory meaningless exercises of divination, waving his hands and chanting gibberish prayers. A fine actor, he pretended that the jewels' location had come suddenly to him in a vision: "Your majesty," he intoned, "you will find the treasure beneath a large boulder.... on the beach!"

Soldiers were dispatched instantly, and the jewels were recovered intact.

The king was overjoyed, and rushed to embrace and reward Harisharam. While the king was drunk with joy and eager to deliver his promised reward, his ministers were somewhat more wary.

"Sire," one minister whispered. "How do we know that this astrologer wasn't one of the thieves? How else could he have known where to find the jewels?"

The king paused and realized that there was truth in the minister's words. Perhaps Harisharam was indeed a fake and a thief.

"We shall test him," the king said in a low voice. He ordered Harisharam to follow him into the royal gardens. ith his back to the others, the king bent to the soil and put a small object in his hand, shielding it from Harisharam's sight.

"Harisharam," the king said. "If you can tell me what I hold in my clenched fist, you will receive your reward. If you cannot, I will have your head cut off."

Once more, Harisharam regretted ever having embarked on this crazy path. He wished he had stayed a foolish but unknown man living squalidly on the village outskirts.

"O Frog," he addressed himself aloud, "you're in a tight spot now!"

The king was agog. He opened his hands and a tiny frog slipped from them, back into the royal gardens. There was a gasp of awe from the assembled observers. Even the suspicious ministers were convinced of Harisharam's authenticity. Again, quick on the recovery, Harisharam smiled deeply and mystically, hoping his shaking knees were imperceptible beneath his coat.

True to his word, the king gave Harisharam riches beyond his dreams. And Harisharam, having learned from this adventure, and having suffered his wife's consternation anew, never attempted to fool anyone ever again.

THE MOST ORNERY HORSE

Tenali Rama was the greatest jester the king's court had ever known. He couldn't dance or juggle, or sing or even play a musical instrument. He told very poor jokes, and refused to dress like a clown or even to suffer the indignities of the courtiers. But he was always able to refute traditional wisdom, and for that the king found him eternally amusing.

One year, the king decided to see which of his wealthy and talented courtiers could develop the finest horse. He granted each of them a fine stallion and enough money to feed the stallion as if it were a king. At this, Tenali Rama shook his head and groaned.

"Is something wrong, Rama?" the king asked.

"Oh, your majesty, once more you are wasting your money. If what you want is strength in an animal, I can give you the most ornery horse possible --without spending a fortune on food or trainers."

At this, the assembled courtiers laughed and demanded to see substance to the jester's words.

The king agreed to give Rama a horse, just like that given to the courtiers. But the jester was given only a few alms with which to buy food for the horse.

Rama immediately set to work. He built a small enclosed pen for the proud stallion, and made a small hole for feeding the animal. Each day for two months, he would push a small handful of dried grass through the hole. And each day, the starving horse would devour his scarce food with desperate abandon.

At the end of the two months, the courtiers brought out their proud animals. One after the next, the stallions blazed with masculine glory, performing great feats of power, speed and raw strength. Finally, it was time for Tenali Rama to unveil his sickly deprived beast.

"Your majesty," Rama said. "I cannot show you my horse because the beast is just too powerful to be told what to do. I and several soldiers tried to pull it from its pen. But it's much too strong for us."

The assembled courtiers laughed again. Clearly, no horse was so powerful!

"This I must see," the king said. "Have the pen brought here in its entirety." His order was fulfilled as several men towed the wooden box to the royal court.

"Royal groom!" the king bellowed to his servant. "Stick your head in that hole and inspect the horse. You have the training to tell a fine beast just by looking at it."

Now, the royal groom was an old man with a very long grey beard. When he stuck his head through the pen's feed hole, the starving horse mistook the groom's beard for its daily ration of dried grass. Not willing to let his meal go by, the horse took hold of the beard and pulled for all his life.

The groom's cries were horrific indeed, and it took all of the soldiers and courtiers to prevent him from being pulled bodily through the feed hole. He was saved... but not his beard.

The king decreed that Tenali Rama had indeed won the contest, and rewarded him richly. Rama, in return, rewarded the horse by setting him free to feast upon a lush meadow for the remainder of his many days.

THE SWEETNESS OF LIES

In ancient times, it was not uncommon for mighty kings to seek philosophical knowledge and perspective from a variety of sources. Greatness, after all, is not only defined by wealth and power, but by understanding and wisdom.

A particularly great king once wished to know what the sweetest taste of all was. While this was perhaps not the most erudite of philosophical queries, it was nonetheless an interesting question that the monarch wished answered. Such are the preoccupations of impressive intellects in times of peace, wealth and excess.

The king considered, who better to ask about sweetness than lovely young women, sweetness incarnate? He thus had his ministers select four young girls from the kingdom, and asked them each, "What do you think is the sweetest taste of all?"

The first girl said, "The taste of meat, O king. Though I am a vegetarian, I've seen animals of all kind fight over scraps of meat. Therefore, meat must be the sweetest thing in the world."

The second girl disagreed. She said, "O king, the sweetest taste is that of wine. Though I've not tasted it, I've seen how the men behave when they've drunk wine. They swoon and laugh, and they do this night after night. Wine must be sweet indeed."

"No, my king," said the third girl. "Love is the sweetest taste. It is from love that children are conceived. After the incredible pain of childbirth, people continue to make love. If it is worth that kind of pain, it must be so very sweet."

The fourth girl, whose name was Kalyani, smiled wickedly. "What is so funny?" the king asked her.

"I fear you may not like my response, Majesty," she said.

"Tell me anyway," the king insisted. "What is the sweetest taste of all?"

"O king," Kalyani said, "the sweetest taste is that of telling lies!"

The king was intrigued. "Go on. What do you mean?"

"Come with me," she said, "and I will show you what I mean." So the king and his two ministers followed Kalyani back to her family's house by the rice fields. Once there, she indicated a solitary hut in the field.

"In that hut," she said, "God himself appears to men who enter alone. But if you are born out of wedlock, and have lived a life of sin, he will not appear to you. Go see."

The king's first minister went first. He stepped into the hut and saw nothing but an empty room. He knew that he was born into wedlock, but was concerned that others might think him a sinful bastard if he couldn't see God here. So, when he emerged, he announced, "I saw God!"

The second minister experienced the same compulsion. For fear of a dishonourable reputation, he too declared that he had seen God inside the hut, though he had seen nothing at all. When the king finally entered, he was alarmed to see nothing but the hut walls. But since his ministers had seen God, people would think him a bastard and a sinner if he told the truth. Predictably, the king announced that he, as well, had seen the image of God inside the hut.

"Liars!" the girl shouted. "You all lied, all three of you! If men as powerful, fearless and honourable as yourselves have lied, then lying must be a sweet taste indeed!"

The king had a good laugh. He was so impressed by the Kalyani's cleverness that he married her and made her his chief advisor.

THE LOST CAMEL

A merchant discovered, much to his dismay, that one of his camels had wandered off into the desert at night. As a camel is a valuable commodity, this was no small loss. The merchant resigned himself to searching out the camel, despite the unlikelihood of ever finding it. The desert is vast, after all, and things lost in the sands tend to remain lost for an eternity.

On the desert at the same time were four wise men travelling from a foreign state to the merchant's land. During their voyage, they came upon signs of a camel's travels. Being thoughtful scholars, they made a game of determining the camel's characteristics strictly from the signs that it left behind.

Eventually, the desperate merchant came upon the four men. "Dear sirs," he said. "Have you seen my lost camel?"

"Was your camel lame?" asked the first wise man.

"Yes. Where is it?" replied the merchant.

"And was your camel blind in one eye?" asked the second wise man.

"Yes, yes. Where is it?"

"Did your camel have an unusually short tail?" asked the third wise man.

"Yes, kind sir. Now please where is my camel?"

"One more thing," said the fourth wise man. "Did your camel suffer from strange internal body pains?"

"Yes!" cried the merchant, now convinced that these men had taken his camel. "Now where is it?"

"We are sorry," the men said. "We've not seen your camel, only its signs. I don't think you'll be able to find it in this vast desert. Best you come with us back to your city."

Now, the merchant was sure these men had stolen and sold his camel. He was intent on bringing them to justice, so agreed to accompany them back to the city.

Once the five of them returned to the city, the merchant summoned guards and had the four wise men arrested. They were shocked, of course, but were in no position to offer protest in a foreign land.

All five were brought before the king. After having been briefed, the thoughtful king said, "It is clear to me that you four have indeed stolen this man's camel. Otherwise how could you know these things about it?"

"Its footprints were heavier on one side than the other," the first wise man said hastily, "so I knew it had to be lame."

"And the berries on the left of the prints had been eaten, but not those on the right," said the second wise man, "so I deduced that it was blind in one eye."

"There were tiny spots of blood on the sand," continued the third blind man. "Clearly, the poor beast was pestered by gnats and flies. Its short tail must have been a poor swatter indeed."

"And I noticed how the front prints were deeper than the rear prints," the last wise man said, "as if its body was contracted by internal pain."

At this re-telling both the king and merchant were duly impressed by the traveller's skills of deduction. Fortunately, the king was himself a wise and fair man, and agreed to recompensed the merchant for his lost camel, and to hire the wise men on as his private advisors.

The fate of the camel, though, remained a secret known only to the whispering desert winds.

O LUCKY RABBIT

A devious and untrustworthy monkey befriended a simple rabbit. As the two of them sat by the side of the road, a man came by carrying fresh bananas upon a long pole.

"Listen, friend," the monkey said to the rabbit. "Go run in front of the man. Humans like to eat rabbits. So, he's sure to drop his fruit and chase you. I'll hen grab the fruit and hide it. When you return, we'll share the food!"

The rabbit agreed and did as he was told. Sure enough, the man dropped his bananas and chased the rabbit. The monkey stole the food and climbed a tree where he quickly devoured both his and the rabbit's share. The man finally tired of chasing the rabbit, and was not pleased to find his bananas missing, but went home nonetheless.

The rabbit returned to find the monkey high up in a tree atop a small mountain of banana peels. "I don't believe you ate all of them!" he cried to his false friend.

"Why did you take so long? It's your own fault!" said the monkey.

"Surely you have some more left up there?" the rabbit begged.

"Come see," said the monkey. He reached down and grabbed the poor rabbit by the ears, lifting him up onto the high branch. The monkey then scampered away, abandoning his "friend."

Now, the rabbit was in a fine predicament indeed, for he was much too high up to jump down. In time, an old rhinoceros wandered by and parked himself beneath the tree. There, he sadly died of old age.

This was fortunate for the rabbit, though, for he was able to jump onto the rhinoceros's back and thence onto the ground. He scampered away happily, but hungrily.

Soon he was lost, and it began to rain, causing him to sneeze and cough. He took the first shelter he found: a human tent set up within the forest. Unbeknownst to the rabbit, this was the king's tent, and the king sat in it, keeping court. The rabbit hid beneath the king's chair, but soon was overtaken by a powerful need to sneeze. or a small creature, his sneeze was loud and strong.

"Who dares sneeze in my presence?" the king bellowed. The chair was overturned and the rabbit discovered. "The penalty for such insolence is death, rabbit."

"Your majesty," the rabbit pleaded. "Please don't kill me. If you spare my life, I can lead you to a dead rhinoceros!" The horn of a rhinoceros is a rare and valuable commodity for its importance in medicinal concoctions and religious ritual. The king was naturally eager to lay claim to such a prize, so agreed to the rabbit's offer.

The rabbit led the king to the great beast's corpse. The king was pleased and surprised, and immediately bent to the task of removing the rhino's horn. The precious find was then placed within the royal treasury.

The king was so pleased with the rabbit that he gave the little animal all the riches he could ever need or want.

The rabbit was content to lounge atop his regal silken blankets and consume all manner of expensive imported vegetables. Some days later, the foul monkey came upon his old acquaintance in all his new regal finery. Where did you get all this?" he demanded.

"From the king," the rabbit said. "I hid under his chair and sneezed. When the king found me, he gave me all of this stuff."

The monkey was insanely jealous. He could sneeze, too, and surely much better than a worthless rabbit. He sped off to the king's tent and cached himself beneath the monarch's chair. When he heard the king sit down, he immediately sneezed as loud as he could.

The king threw aside the chair and grasped the monkey by his neck. "What can you offer me, monkey, that I should not cut off your head for such insolence?"

"Um," the monkey said, "I have a big pile of banana peels?" With that answer, the pathetic monkey's fate was sealed.

THE MAGIC
RICE PADDY

Subodh was an orphan who had but one possession: a small rice paddy that he cultivated diligently for his sustenance. But this paddy was odd -- the rice grew at such a phenomenal rate, that it was impossible to finish harvesting its yield. Subodh would begin its harvest, and the rice would re-grow behind him. This was a boon, certainly, but a frustrating one.

One day, the seven vain but beautiful daughters of the Rajah were picking berries in the forest adjacent to Subodh's little rice paddy. When they saw him and his field, they called out: "You must be the laziest and ugliest man in the country! Why can't you harvest this one little field?"

"I'm trying!" Subodh protested. "Every time I start, the rice grows back right behind me!" At this, the girls laughed aloud and mocked poor Subodh. "Look," he said to them. "You don't believe me? I'll pick berries for you, and you can try to harvest my rice. If you finish my harvest before I can fill all of your baskets, you may take me with you as your slave. But if I complete the picking first, you must all agree to be my wives!"

The girls were horrified by the thought of marrying such an inconsequential individual. But they were certain that they could harvest the little paddy in mere minutes, and it would be fine to have a pathetic little slave like Subodh. So they agreed.

Subodh went into the forest and, in the course of a few hours, managed to fill all seven baskets with berries. The girls, on the other hand, bent to their task gleefully, but rapidly became frustrated when their harvesting could not keep up with the rice's magical rate of re-growth. When Subodh returned with the seven baskets, the girls knew they had lost the bet.

But they refused to marry him, insisting that deals made with commoners weren't binding under the law.

Feeling cheated, Subodh rightly protested. Being poor and ugly, he was concerned that this might be his only chance to have a family; and he was not about to let it slip by him. He insisted that they take the case to the girls' father, the Rajah.

When the Rajah heard of the predicament, he was not pleased. Subodh was not a prince, and therefore not an appropriate choice of husband for his royal daughters. However, the Rajah was respectful of the kingdom's laws, and realized that his family must set a good example by always keeping their word. Reluctantly, he commanded that his seven beautiful daughters all become wed to young Subodh.

Subodh was overjoyed, of course. But, on his wedding night, his new wives had other ideas. They permitted him to sleep with them, but allowed him no carnal knowledge. Theirs was to be a polygamous marriage in name alone, with none of the bodily pleasures that marriages usually entail.

Subodh was at a loss. His dream of a family was to be denied him, after all.

Some days later, Subodh returned to his little rice paddy and spied a wild macaque destroying the crop. He managed to capture the monkey. But it inadvertently died of fright when Subodh wrapped his hands around it. Oddly, that breed of macaque has a tendency to display an erect penis when frightened, and, sure enough, the dead monkey brandished a stiff and intrusive male organ.

Subodh struck upon an idea.

He brought the corpse of the monkey back to the palace and pretended to conceal it from his wives. Always wary of their husband, the princesses immediately wrested the monkey from Subodh. They found its anatomy fascinating to say the least. "What do you think it died of?" they asked.

"Obviously," Subodh said, "It died of too much sex. The males of this species of macaque take many wives, and so often drop dead of too much physical love. The same has happened to several of my male relatives: all dead from too much carnal knowledge."

Predictably, the princesses conspired amongst themselves. They would kill their hated husband with too much love! That night, and for several subsequent nights, they took turns ravishing the grateful Subodh who stubbornly refused to die from the treatment.

Nine months later, all seven of the foolish girls gave birth to Subodh's sons and daughters. His dream came true, after all.

THE FOOLISH POTMAKER AND THE TIGER

This is the story of how a silly potmaker became renowned throughout the kingdom as a brave and ferocious man.

One evening, as the first touches of the Indian monsoons arrived at a small village, a great and terrible tiger crouched in the shade of a tree by a potmaker's house. Tigers are those rare animals who understand human speech, though their vocabulary suffers somewhat. So from his proximity, this particular tiger was able to hear and understand the chattering of the potmaker's wife inside the house.

The potmaker was yet to arrive home, though the sun had set, and his wife was cursing both her husband's absence and the annoying rain that dripped through the hut's thatched roof. "This dreadful dripping!' she cried aloud, "How I detest this dreadful dripping!"

Now this was a term the tiger had never heard before.

"What is a 'dreadful dripping'?" he asked himself, and strained to hear more to solve this mystery.

The potmaker's wife was becoming livid as her belongings slowly began to get damp. She was particularly concerned for her wooden chairs and chests which might become warped should they get wet. As these items constituted a fair portion of her dowry, she was rightfully terrified that they would be ruined. "You dreadful dripping!" she cried again. "I fear you more than I fear the beasts of the forest!"

At this, the tiger became alarmed. If the potmaker's wife was more afraid of this "dreadful dripping" than she was of wild beasts --even of tigers!-- then this strange thing must be terrible indeed!

The potmaker's wife was desperate to save her wooden things. Frantically, she pushed her heavy chairs and chests along the floor, hoping to get them out of the way of the streams of water now snaking across her floor. This created an awful noise as the furniture dragged along the hard floor, and the tiger's ears bristled.

"That awful sound," he said to himself, "must be the sound of the 'dreadful dripping'!"

Just then, as the rain began to fall in thick blinding sheets, the potmaker himself arrived home. His donkey had become loose from the cart. But, because his vision was blurred, the potmaker could barely make out animals from people and trees.

Seeing the figure of the tiger sitting by the house, the potmaker assumed it was his donkey. He lunged at the blurry figure, slapping the beast's back and sides with the flats of his hands.

"You horrible animal," the potmaker reprimanded, "get back to the post so I can tie you up!"

The tiger was rather surprised at this turn of events. First, he had heard the noise of this dreadful dripping, and now he was being struck with considerable force. Surely, this fierce man was the dreadful dripping that the woman feared so much. With this revelation, the tiger was much too frightened to fight back, and agreed to be tied to the donkey post.

In the morning, when the rain had stopped, the villagers gathered outside the potmaker's house to see the incredible sight. The most ferocious beast of the forest, it was seen, had been wrestled into submission by the brave and powerful potmaker. His reputation as a great hero was assured.

THE POTMAKER
AND THE ARMY

As tended to happen in India's ancient past, one kingdom was preparing to invade another. The Rajah of the kingdom that was being attacked was, of course, quite alarmed. Not being a great military leader himself, he needed to find someone to do the job for him. Certainly, he had many brave and qualified generals who could rise to the task, but none of them possessed the charisma and popular support that was needed to inspire a conscripted army of farmers and merchants.

In one of the villages of that kingdom, however, lived our friend the potmaker. As his reputation for having wrestled and bested a wild tiger spread, the people came to demand that the potmaker be appointed leader of the army. Only a man as brave and as strong as a tiger can best a tiger, they reasoned, and only a tiger is suited to defend the kingdom from invasion.

The silly potmaker had, by this time, begun to believe these ridiculous stories about himself. When he looked at his reflection now, he didn't see a scrawny, bald old man, but a muscular young warrior with bright eyes, ebony locks and a magnificent chest. So, he took to his new post as general with a vigour.

"The first thing I'll need to do," he told the Rajah, "Is to observe the enemy position."

"Excellent," the Rajah said. "I'll make you a gift of my finest stallion."

Now, the potmaker had never before ridden a horse, and was not so clouded in his vainglory that he would forget this very important fact.

"Oh no, my king," he protested. "A small pony would be best. I don't want the enemy to hear the gallops of a mighty stallion."

But, much to the potmaker's dismay, the Rajah had delivered to him an enormous white war stallion raging for a fight.

The potmaker turned to his wife for advice. It was clear that this magnificent beast would throw the inexperienced rider straight away, thus erasing the potmaker's ill-gotten reputation. His wife paced for a few moments, then struck upon an idea: "We'll tie you to its back!"

Before he could offer a reasonable protest, the potmaker found himself sitting atop the stallion's back. Seeing the animal snort and tremble, as if its patience were being tested, the potmaker's wife worked rapidly. She tied her husband's legs and feet to the stirrups, and lashed his thighs to the saddle. Just as she finished, the stallion reared up on its hind legs, then bolted toward the forest.

"Wife!" the potmaker called, his torso flailing dangerously. "You forgot to tie my hands!"

"Grab onto its mane!" she shouted back. The potmaker complied, and clung to the mighty beast's mane for dear life.

The stallion galloped straight through the forest, and was heading directly for the invading army who had made camp on an adjacent plain. Upon realizing this, the potmaker was frantic. He tried everything to slow the stallion, knowing a noisy entrance would surely mean his death.

When nothing was working, he reached out and wrapped his arms around a banyan tree.

Now, due to the power of the horse, the looseness of the soil, and the rottenness of the tree's roots, the potmaker actually managed to pull the entire tree from the ground! He was now galloping at full tilt toward the enemy position, tree in hand.

Upon seeing this sight, the enemy soldiers were stricken with terror. "The enemy army is coming!" they cried. "And it is lead by a giant so strong he can rip whole trees from the ground!"

The invaders panicked, and ran about in disarray. Finally, the enemy general screamed from the melee, "We surrender! Please don't kill us!"

Somehow, the potmaker managed to get the stallion turned around and headed back toward the village. Halfway there, the stallion ran out of steam, and the slow trot back took hours.

When they finally reached the village, the potmaker screamed at his wife to cut him free. "I may not get another chance to get off this terrible horse! Do it now!"

Finally back on his own two feet, the potmaker stumbled clumsily to the Rajah's palace. But a messenger from the enemy had already come and gone, and the kingdom was once more at peace.

"Look at this man," the Rajah said of the approaching potmaker. "He defeats an enemy army singlehandedly, and is still so modest that he walks to his king, rather than ride atop his stallion."

And with the people's raucous approval, the potmaker was made first minister of the kingdom.

THE POSSESSED WIFE

There once was a nimble village man who loved to eat fish and mangoes. On the outskirts of his village, there was a temple dedicated to Kali, a Hindu goddess. On the grounds of this temple was a pond filled with glorious carp, as well as an orchard of healthy mango trees.

According to the law of the land, however, plants and animals that grow on temple grounds are not to be eaten. Anyone caught doing so was punished most harshly. Of course, the village man desired both the bright orange temple fish and the succulent mangoes that grew in such divine protection.

After weeks of considering his options, he finally devised a plan. He sauntered casually by the temple. And with his long hand and his dexterous foot, he both picked a mango and caught a fish at the same time. He flipped both items into his sack, and quickly scurried home, certain that no one had seen him commit this crime.

The village man was very excited to present his stolen gains to his wife, who was equally as sly. She had no qualms against eating illegal food, and immediately set about cooking the fish and mango together.

The combination of the two foods was a delicacy in these parts. Both the man and his wife swooned in anticipation when the odour of the meal reached their nostrils. The man was impatient to eat the delicious meal, but decided to distract himself by working in his garden. His wife had no choice, however, but to remain with the pan of food as it cooked, tempted by its wonderful odour.

As she added various spices, she needed to taste the

fish and fruit from time to time. It was indeed a marvellous combination, and she tasted more and more. After a few minutes, to her horror, she realized she had eaten the whole meal!

From behind her, she heard her husband returning from the garden. "That smells so good!" he sang. "I can't wait to taste that fish!"

The wife began to panic. Her husband would be furious when he found she had eaten the whole meal. She thought quickly, bringing that devious mind of hers into full play. She put a lid on top of the empty pan, and ruffled her hair and clothes.

"How dare you steal from my temple!" she bellowed to her husband.

"What?" he cried. "What are you saying?"

"It is I, the goddess Kali," the wife said. "I have taken possession of this woman's body so that you might know my displeasure!"

The man dropped to his knees in terror, his lips quivering and his limbs shaking.

"O Kali," he pleaded, "Forgive me! I was foolish. I promise to never do such crimes again."

"Indeed you shall not," the wife said in regal tones. "This is what you must do to earn my forgiveness..."

"I will do anything to avoid your wrath!"

"Take the fish and the mango back to the temple grounds," she said, handing her husband the covered pan. "Drop the pan into the fish pond. You will see that instantly, the fish you have killed and cooked will return to life and swim away. And the mango you have callously picked will spring back onto the branches of the tree. Then, and only then, will you be forgiven."

"Yes, yes," the frightened man said. "Anything."

"And you must not look in the pan. If you do, both you and this woman will be destroyed. Go now."

The man leapt to his feet and ran back to the temple. Following the instructions perfectly, he dropped the pan into the pond, careful not to look directly into the pan. As no fried fish or cooked mango sank to the bottom of the pond, he saw it as a miracle. He fished out the empty pan and returned it to his wife, much relieved to find that she was no longer possessed by the terrible goddess Kali.

Needless to say, he never tried to steal from a goddess again.

The wife went to bed happily that night, and left her husband to fill his belly with legally earned rice.

THE PUMPKIN AND
THE WALNUT

Manish was a foolish man indeed. Like most foolish men, he thought himself to be wise beyond his years.

One day, like most days, he found himself staring blankly into the garden. There were no thoughts in his head, profound or otherwise. But he felt his continence to be one of utmost sagacity: meditative and guru-like.

On this day, he spied two growths that took his fancy: a walnut tree and a pumpkin grove.

Wishing to impress the onlooking vegetation with a fine display of contemplative might, he posited, "Why should such a large thing --the pumpkin-- have such small seeds? And why should such a small thing --the walnut-- have such a large seed? This is a most foolish arrangement indeed. The forces of nature would be better served to reverse this arrangement!"

Now, the local wiseman had observed Manish for some months, and was usually content to let the boy stew in his own confusion. But this was quite the arrogant declaration indeed. To question the wisdom of the forces of nature is to invite retribution.

Sitting almost invisibly within the pumpkin grove, the wiseman called upon his many years of study. He closed his eyes and concentrated on the appropriate spells, incantations and invocations. The result, after many minutes of such work, was that the walnut tree was now heavy with pumpkins hanging from its branches, while the grove was peppered with hundreds of walnuts with tiny seeds.

"Much better!" declared Manish, pleased to see that his advice had been taken. "You will find, O Nature, that this is a much better arrangement."

And with that, a pumpkin fell from the walnut tree and smacked Manish hard on the skull. He never again questioned the wisdom of nature.

THE FOUR STORIES

India is a land that revels in its oral traditions, and so travelling Storytellers were historically valued in the small rural communities. There was one such Storyteller who relied on only four stories to satisfy his audiences. He told the same four stories everywhere he went. But he told them so cleverly that they seemed new each time; and no one else, despite their attempts, could ever tell them the same way.

The Storyteller finally took on an Apprentice who was eager to learn these stories. But the Storyteller would not teach the stories to his student just yet. Instead, he felt it was important for the Apprentice to earn the right to learn these stories by working as a servant for some months.

The Apprentice was not happy with this arrangement, and was impatient to learn these four stories as well as the special way to recite them. So, one night when the Storyteller was asleep, the Apprentice lay awake next to him to await the emergence of the stories.

Sure enough, one by one, the four stories crawled out of the Storyteller's navel and sat atop his belly. They were small and multicoloured, with grim little faces and bulbous little heads. The Apprentice shut his eyes hard in mock sleep, but listened as the stories conversed.

The first story said, "This is a fine Storyteller in whom we live. But he never lets anyone else know how to tell us! I feel useless living in his belly!"

"Agreed," said the second story. "What should we do about it?"

"We should kill him!" shouted the third story. The

Apprentice almost gasped aloud, but remained silent for fear of discovery.

"Yes," said the fourth story. "But how shall we kill him?"

"Hmmm," the first story pondered. "When the Storyteller eats his first mouthful of food in the morning, I'll turn it into a mouthful of needles! So when he swallows, the needles will kill him!"

"That's good," the second story agreed. "But if that doesn't work, I'll knock over the big tree by the roadside. When he walks by, the tree will fall on him, and he will be crushed!"

The third story giggled in delight, but was concerned for the failure of both plans. "Well if that doesn't work, I'll turn into a poisonous snake, run up his leg and bite him!"

"And I," finished the fourth story, "will summon a great wave of water tomorrow as the Storyteller is crossing the river, and he will be drowned!"

The four stories laughed fiendishly, then returned through the Storyteller's navel to continue hatching their plot. The Apprentice was concerned, of course, and resolved to protect his master.

The next morning at breakfast, just as the Storyteller was about to take his first mouthful of food, the Apprentice leapt forward and shouted, "There's a scorpion in your bowl!" He snatched the food from his master, and tossed it away, saving the Storyteller from the deadly needles.

Breakfast continued uneventfully. Afterward, the two continued on their journey, and the Apprentice spotted the great tree in the distance. Playfully, he said to the Storyteller, "Master, let us race past the tree to the end of the road!"

The Storyteller was not one to shrink from a challenge, so agreed. The two sped past the great tree just as it fell, missing them both.

Up ahead, the wary Apprentice spotted the snake summoned by the third story. He raced ahead with his staff and beat the snake away, saving his master from its deadly bite. nd when the pair came upon the river to be crossed, the Apprentice remembered the fourth story's promise to drown them. He pleaded with the Storyteller to take the high bridge across, and not to wade across the shallow part.

The Storyteller finally agreed, and the two crossed safely to the other side, just as a mighty wave roared passed them.

The Storyteller was an old man, but not unaware. He had noticed the transpired events, and realized that his servant had been protecting him. "How were you aware of these threats?" he demanded of the Apprentice.

Cowed, the Apprentice confessed to having eavesdropped while the stories had conspired. The Storyteller laughed aloud, patted the Apprentice on the back, and declared, "That's the best story of all!"

The Storyteller was so pleased that that night he taught the Apprentice the stories and how to tell them. And with such mastery, the two of them were easily able to control the fiendish little stories, who now knew better than to try to take on two great Storytellers.

KILLED BY A TIGER

A village man received word that his sister, who lived in a neighbouring village, was about to give birth to her first child. Wanting to be present at the moment of birth, the fellow set out on the overnight journey to his sister's village.

On the way, he stopped to rest by a large banyan tree. Wary of wild animals, he felt it safest to sleep in the branches of the great tree, well above the reach of the vicious tigers who patrolled this land.

After some hours, he was wakened by the sound of two tigers conversing beneath him. He kept very quiet and listened to their conversation, for one can often learn much from the wisdom of wild beasts.

Now, tt was well known that tigers could foretell the time and manner of a person's death, and that was indeed the topic of their conversation.

"A boy is being born in the village tonight," the first tiger said.

"Yes, I know," replied the second tiger. "He will die on his wedding day, won't he?"

"Mmmm, yes. He will be killed by one of our brothers, another tiger, on the very day of his marriage." In agreement, the two tigers strolled off into the forest.

The village man was horrified. His nephew was to be murdered by a tiger many years hence! He vowed to keep vigil over the boy, from now until his wedding day, so that he might slay this prophesied tiger before it could do its damage.

Many years passed, and the boy grew into a fine young man. True to his word, the uncle kept by him, always ready with his knife and spear lest a tiger leap from the bush. The nephew matured to adulthood, and in time a suitable bride was selected for him. Arrangements were made for his marriage, and the uncle knew that the dreaded day had finally come.

The uncle made sure he would accompany his nephew on the groom's procession to the ceremony. He gripped his weapons at the ready, knowing that a wild beast was due to appear. On schedule, an enormous tiger leapt from behind a tree and threw itself upon the young groom.

But the uncle was prepared. ith great skill and preparedness, he brandished his knife and slew the tiger cleanly, thus saving his nephew's life.

The wedding went smoothly, and, that night, the man confessed to his sister and nephew the details of his foreknowledge. Naturally, they were both very grateful for his diligence, and had the tiger's head brought before them so that they could contemplate the tragedy they had so narrowly escaped.

"So this was the tiger that was supposed to kill me, eh?" the brash young groom said. "Take that!" He levelled a vicious kick against the dead animal's head.

Clumsily, though, he struck the dead tiger's great teeth, and sliced his foot open. The wound bled profusely, and no one could seal it.

The young man bled to death that very night, and the tigers' prophecy was sadly fulfilled.

THE RIDDLE OF
THE WILL

In the vast province called Rajasthan, there once lived a fair and wise man named Amar. Like most men of the region, Amar was a farmer and cattle tender who had accumulated, through many years of diligence and hard work, a comfortable amount of wealth with which to raise his family. Amar was also in possession of an agile wit, and was fond of puzzles, riddles and parables. He often plied his sons' intellects with symbolic tests and other displays of wit and sagacity.

As a man of forethought, Amar was concerned for the disposition of his property once he departed this mortal domain. So, as is still the custom in most of the world, Amar contemplated the writing of a will.

He had three young sons who would one day be men, and who would surely raise families of their own. It was the practice of the day for sons to live their lives under their father's roof, raising their own families there for many generations. Amar was concerned about the possibility of change. A day may come, for instance, when his sons would choose to separate their families and go their separate ways.

How then to fairly divide the family's communal possessions among them? This was the issue that consumed him for many days, until finally he gathered his young boys to him.

"My sons," Amar said. "Many years from now --or tomorrow! -- when I am dead, all of my possessions will be yours. It is my hope that you all will continue to live here, with your wives and children and grandchildren, and work the lands together as brothers."

The boys nodded, though they were somewhat taken aback by the topic of conversation and by the gravity of their father's countenance.

"However," Amar continued, "there may come a time when the three of you will wish to separate from each other. When that time comes, I want you to dig immediately below where I am sitting now. In this spot I have left a will that will detail a fair manner of dividing the wealth."

At that, Amar made his sons swear to him that they would follow the will if that time ever came. He then put the matter out of his mind for the rest of his life.

Amar lived a long life indeed, eventually embracing his gods at a ripe old age, leaving behind his grown sons and their wives and children.

Many years passed while the three brothers tended their father's land, raised his cattle and invested his gold. Their ministrations proved sufficiently profitable to garner their individual families a comfortable existence, and there were few quarrels.

There came a time, however, as their own children began to grow older, that minor conflicts began to erupt between the three families. Petty matters concerning space and personal habits began to nag at them, slowly transforming the estate into an unpleasant place to live.

So the brothers gathered to discuss the inevitable: they would dig up their late father's will and decide how best to divide their communal wealth. They had marked the location many years ago, so had no trouble finding the will's burial spot. But what they pulled up after hours of digging was quite a surprise. Instead of a document, they unearthed three clay pots packed into a box. Filled in the first pot was loose earth; in the second pot, there were random bones, presumably from dead cows. And in the third were a few pieces of coal.

What did this mean? They remembered their father's

cryptic ways, and realized immediately that this was some kind of riddle, his final posthumous test of his sons' cleverness. They sat in contemplation for many hours, but could make no headway in the puzzle. Several days passed, and still they were no closer to a solution. After a week, they agreed to seek outside consultation, and went to the village elders.

"O ancient ones," the eldest son said to the gathered elders. "We are aware of your wisdom and cleverness, and so defer to your judgement as to the meaning of these three pots."

The elders were flattered indeed, and, in their arrogance, were convinced that they would have a solution in a matter of minutes. But many days passed again, and even the elders had no solution.

The problem was then opened to the entire family who gathered nightly to ponder the riddle. It proved a point of great contention, but also a subject of considerable amusement, particularly for the children. But no solution was forthcoming.

Later that season, word came of a wise hermit living in the forest outside the town of Udaipur, a place renowned for its production of sages and ascetics. Eager to put the matter of the will to rest, the three sons gathered their travelling clothes, and set off together to see the hermit.

After days of journeying and inquiring, they came upon the hermit's hovel and explained their problem to him. The hermit laughed a loud and hearty laugh.

"If only you'd taken some time to think about it, you'd have saved yourself a trip!" the hermit exclaimed.

"But we *did* think about it!" the sons protested.

"Clearly not! Look, the pot of earth says that one of you -- the eldest, I would think-- should own the land. The pot of cow bones says that another should own the cattle. And the pot of coal indicates mineral wealth, that the last son should receive whatever gold your father owned. A fair division indeed!"

The riddle of the will was indeed solved. But a queer thing happened. In contemplating the problem, the families of the three sons were thrown closer together than they had been before, and discovered, much to their surprise, that they didn't want to separate after all!

WISDOM FOR SALE

There once was a poor man who owned nothing except his excellent mind. Still, one must eat, and he was compelled to find a trade from which to earn a living. Seeing how the merchants profitably sold wares and goods in the bazaar, the wise man struck upon an idea. He set up a booth in the bazaar, and put up a sign: "Wisdom for sale -- one rupee."

In time, a young boy happened by. This boy was from a wealthy family, but was not particularly smart. He saw the odd sign and immediately deposited one rupee in the wiseman's cup. The wiseman scribbled a sentence on a piece of paper, "Do not watch two people fighting," and gave it to his customer.

That night, the wealthy boy showed his new purchase to his father. The father was enraged, of course, and the next day he marched his son back to the bazaar to confront the wiseman. "You have cheated my son," he said. "Take back your paper. I want my rupee back!"

"Certainly," the wiseman said. "You will have your rupee back. But I didn't sell your son a piece of paper. I sold him *wisdom*. In exchange for my rupee, your son must swear that he will not use this piece of wisdom."

"How can he do this?" the father asked.

"Whenever two people are fighting, he *must* stay and watch!" The gathered onlookers agreed that this was an equitable situation, so both the father and the son conceded, as well, to the wise man's condition.

Some time later, two wealthy women came to the bazaar to shop. As their husbands were rivals, the two women quickly entered into a quarrel. The silly boy, remembering his father' agreement with the wiseman, stood diligently watching the fight. When the king's soldiers came to break up the altercation, they noticed that the boy had witnessed the whole affair. As was their duty, they commanded the boy to attend the king's court the following morning to bear witness as to the nature of this quarrel.

Now, the two quarrelling women were quite devious. Wishing to prepare as strong a case as possible, they each in turn approached the boy and threatened to cut his head off if he did not offer a biased testimony before the king.

The boy's father was desperate. Naturally, he was concerned for his son's life, but did not know what to do! At last, he resolved to seek the advice from the wiseman in the bazaar. Once more with his foolish son in tow, he hurried to the wise man's booth.

"I see your problem," the wiseman said, after having been briefed. "Your solution will cost you 500 rupees"

The wealthy man was appalled, but had little choice. He paid the 500 rupees.

"Now," the wiseman said. "When your son goes to court tomorrow, he must speak only in random syllables. That way, the king will think him insane and the boy will be excused from having to give testimony."

"Brilliant!" the father exclaimed, and rushed home to prepare his son. They followed the wise man's plan perfectly, and, as predicted, the king threw the boy out of his court, convinced that the idiot was indeed mad. Later that day, however, the father returned to the wise man in the bazaar.

"Wiseman," he said, "Your plan worked, but now my son must pretend to be mad all the time. If the king finds out he was pretending, he would surely cut off his head!"

"Not a problem," the wiseman answered. "For one thousand rupees I will tell you what to do."

Once more, the father gave over the sum as requested.

The wiseman told him: "Your son must wait several days until the king is in a good mood, then he must go to the palace and explain everything from the beginning. The king will appreciate his honesty, and will have a good laugh."

Reluctantly, the father instructed his foolish son to follow these instructions. As the wiseman had said, the king was fair and wise, and accepted the story in good humour. The king was quite intrigued by the tale, and especially by the existence of a dispenser of advice. "This man in the bazaar must be wise indeed," the king was heard to remark. "Perhaps I should pay him a visit."

Some days later, the royal caravan stopped in the bazaar, and the king himself emerged to speak with the wiseman. All were silent and respectful, fearful of the reason for this royal visit. The wiseman merely raised an eyebrow and waited. "What wisdom will you offer me?" the king asked him at last.

"My words, O king, will cost you one hundred thousand rupees," the wiseman answered. There were shocked gasps from the crowd, but the king just laughed. He was, after all, a gloriously rich man, and the sum was easily affordable.

"All right," the king agreed. "But the advice had better be worth it!" He paid the fare, and the wiseman handed over another piece of paper. On it was written: "Think deeply before every action."

The king thought for a moment, then conceded that this was indeed sage, if somewhat obvious, advice, and he ordered the caravan to return him to the palace. That night, however, the wiseman's words lingered in the king's mind, echoing with prophetic truth. He became so obsessed with the phrase that he had it engraved onto the side of his favourite drinking cup.

Now, it so happened that there had been brewing a plot to assassinate the king. Both his first minister and his private physician had been conspiring for many days to poison the monarch and thence to usurp his throne. Finally, the day of their action was upon them, and the plan began to take unfold. The physician brought to the king his nightly sip of warm milk, but in it was a deadly poison extracted from a venomous snake.

As the king lifted the cup to sip from it, he saw the engraved message on its side: "Think deeply before every action." So, he paused and pondered the situation. "Here," he said to the physician. "You drink it."

Of course, the physician refused, and in time he confessed to his plan. Both he and the minister were imprisoned for their treachery, while the wiseman of the bazaar was offered the job of first minister.

From pauper to wealthy minister, the wiseman had risen solely through the sagacity of his own mind.

THE FOUR UNWISE WISEMEN

There were once four wisemen who had spent their many decades travelling through the vast land, accruing arcane knowledge of all kinds. Their voyages had granted them honour, respect, genuine ability and power.

But what they lacked was certainty.

"How do I know that my abilities are true?" one wiseman asked the others. "What point is there in being stuffed with knowledge, but having no opportunity to exercise it?" The others agreed, but could think of no solution to their conundrum.

Finally, in the forest they came upon the aged and decayed thighbone of a tiger. "Listen" said the first wiseman," with my powers, I can recreate the entire skeleton of this beast!"

The others agreed that this would be a fine display of his practical knowledge. So, he went to work, reciting spells, brewing concoctions, and forging materials from vegetation and rock. In a few hours, he had indeed recreated and assembled the entire skeleton of the great tiger.

"That gives me an idea," said the second wiseman. "With my powers, I can fashion the internal organs of this departed beast." He set to work, invoking the appropriate magic words, and inscribing the necessary secret phrases upon parchment. The result, some hours later, was the skinless and lifeless tiger, standing eerily upon the grass.

"My task," said the third wiseman, "is to give the beast its skin, fur and colours." This required the wiseman to look into the past, to divine what scars and markings the tiger had had in life. Sure enough, the third wiseman succeeded, and the tiger's skin and fur were restored.

The fourth wiseman was the greatest among them. "What is left to me," he declared, "is to give the beast life."

They all breathed deeply, for the skill required to perform this last feat was indeed immense. The fourth wiseman summoned unearthly energies, calling down lightning strikes, and bringing forth gale-force winds from the four directions.

Finally, the spark of life was again lit within the tiger's heart, and it burst to life. It looked around, saw the four wisemen, and ate them all.

SAVRITRI & SATYAVAN

There once was a lovely young princess named Savritri who, by all accounts, was the most perfect daughter a king could raise. Not only was Savritri smart and lovely, with bright eyes and flawless skin, but she displayed great sympathy for all living things, tending to the royal gardens and helping to raise the palace pets.

As she grew, so did her reverence for life. She became a vegetarian and convinced her father to discontinue his regular hunting trips. She became known throughout the kingdom as a great soul, a woman whose wisdom and kindness could always be counted upon. It was said that even the gods were impressed by Savritri's goodness. It was not surprising, then, that all of the eligible princes of the region desired Savritri's hand in marriage.

This was a time when young women of royal birth were encouraged to select their own husbands, and were not required to accept the men that her parents chose for her. In keeping with this tradition, Savritri's father convinced her to travel to a nearby kingdom to visit with the princes there, and to perhaps find a suitable husband.

So, Savritri assembled a royal caravan to undertake the long voyage to the neighbouring kingdom. On the way there, however, the caravan came upon a blind man and his son. The two had apparently been living in the forest for some time. This was not unusual since, at this time, many wisemen chose to live in the forest away from the distractions of regular life.

The blind man's tale was surprising, however. It seemed that he was in fact a king of a distant realm that had been destroyed by an invading army. Since his kingdom no longer existed, the old blind king had decided to live as an ascetic, a holy recluse, with his only son.

When Princess Savritri looked upon the blind king's son, Satyavan, she felt her heart might stop. Satyavan was a terribly handsome young man with broad powerful shoulders and princely long hair that fell to the small of his muscular back. Conversation with Satyavan was as deep and as important as the talks she had with her closest friends, and she could sense in him the same reverence for life that she displayed. It was clear to her that she could easily love this man.

Savritri cancelled her journey and returned to her father's kingdom with her two guests in tow.

Her father was happy to receive guests, and tended to them as would any good host. Meanwhile, Savritri began the preparations for a royal wedding. In these times, it was typical for a young woman to seek guidance from a *rishi*, a very wise holy man, when embarking on an important event, such as a marriage. Savritri found a *rishi* of good reputation, one who had advised her father well on many occasions, and asked the wiseman if her choice of husband was a good one.

"Yes, Princess," the *rishi* responded. "Prince Satyavan will be an excellent husband. He will be faithful and loving, and will bring great honour to your family." Savritri was warmed by this news. "However," the *rishi* continued, "Satyavan is cursed. He is destined to die exactly twelve months from this day."

Savritri was horrified. Had fate delivered to her a perfect husband, only to steal him away after just a year? But, once again, her goodness shone through. She would not let this prophecy deter her from what she knew was right. She announced that the wedding would proceed, but vowed to never let Satyavan know anything of this prediction.

Satyavan and Savritri were married the very next day, and there was much celebration in the kingdom. The newlyweds were very happy together, and were almost never apart. As the months passed, their love for one another grew in great bounds, and it was clear to all that they were, in fact, meant to be together.

All too soon, the day of Satyavan's prophesied death

arrived. As Satyavan had no knowledge of the *rishi*'s words, he made no objection to joining his wife on a walk through the forest. Savritri, of course, was understandably nervous, not knowing how her husband would meet his demise, or if he would suffer unduly.

Satyavan soon began complaining of a headache, and grew tired as they strolled among the trees. "Dear wife," he said to her. "Let me rest here for a while." He lay his head upon her lap, letting his eyes close. Savritri knew that the end was near.

She listened to Satyavan breathe. First, his chest rose and fell as it usually did. Then, his breath grew shallower and less frequent, until finally stopping altogether. Savritri felt her eyes well with tears, as she was powerless to help her dying husband.

Just then, the figure of an enormous man appeared before them. He was a head taller than most men, with heavily muscled arms and legs like tree trunks. is lips were as red as the dark clay that lay on the forest floor, and his long black hair was braided into a long tail that dropped to the base of his spine. His eyes glowed with immortal wisdom, and in his hands he held a short noose.

Savritri knew this figure immediately. It was Yama, the god of death.

"Lord Yama," she pleaded to him. "My husband is a good man. Please do not take him from me."

It was Yama's job to take the souls of the dead into the next world. Among the gods, he was well respected for his fairness and compassion. But he was bound by the rules of his station. "I cannot, princess," he said. "Your respect for life is well known to me, which is why I allow myself to be seen by you. But I cannot break the rules for your husband."

Yama reached down then, and drew Satyavan's soul into his hands. He tied his noose around the soul, and proceeded to drag it away. Savritri was desperate to save her husband. She ran alongside the god, trying to keep up with his great strides. "Where he goes, I will go!" she declared loudly.

Yama paid her no mind, but was sympathetic to her pain. Savritri started to lecture the god about many things. She spoke firstly about the importance of piety, of respecting the gods and their rules. Then she spoke of Satyavan's life, how he had sacrificed his future to stay with his blind father. She spoke, too, of Satyavan's father, how he had endured so much that the death of his only son was a further undeserved tragedy. She spoke then of the grandeur of all life, the importance of living all lives to their fullest. And lastly, she spoke of Yama's own greatness and compassion, and especially of his honesty and integrity.

The god of death was moved and flattered by these words, so well spoken and clearly understood. To reward this devotion, he offered to grant Savritri three boons. She could wish for anything at all, except for the life of her husband.

Being a generous and selfless woman, Savritri immediately knew the things for which she must wish. She wished first for Satyavan's father to regain his sight; then she wished for him to regain his lost kingdom. Lastly, she wished that she and Satyavan would have a hundred children.

Yama, true to his word, waved his mighty hand and decreed that all these things should come to pass.

"Ah, but my lord," Savritri said. "How can Satyavan have a hundred children if he is not alive?"

Yama smiled, knowing that he had been outsmarted by the princess. But because he was an honourable god, he kept his word. He dragged Satyavan's soul back to his body, and re-inserted it.

A few hours later, Satyavan awoke from his long sleep to find himself nestled in the loving lap of his talented wife, never knowing of what had transpired. He and Savritri lived long happy lives, raising one hundred children, just as Yama had promised.

❊ ❊ ❊

ABOUT THE AUTHOR

Raywat Deonandan

Raywat Deonandan is a professor at the University of Ottawa, and a highly decorated scholar and writer. In 2000, his first book, "Sweet Like Saltwater," was awarded the Guyana Prize, which is the national book award of the nation of Guyana, in the "Best First Work" category.

Manufactured by Amazon.ca
Bolton, ON